The
HOUSE
on
MAPLE
STREET

The
HOUSE
on
MAPLE
STREET

BONNIE PRYOR
illustrated by
BETH PECK

 A Mulberry Paperback Book, New York

—Bonnie Pryor—
To all children who have wondered about the past

—Beth Peck—
For my husband, Alan, and in the memory of Eva Dansker

Text copyright © 1987 by Bonnie Pryor
Illustrations copyright © 1987 by Beth Peck

Printed in the United States of America.
First Mulberry Edition, 1992.
9 10

Library of Congress Cataloging-in-Publication Data
Pryor, Bonnie.
The House on Maple Street.
Summary: During the course of three hundred years, many people have passed by or lived on the spot now occupied by a house numbered 107 Maple Street.
[1. Time–Fiction.   2. Change–Fiction]   I. Peck, Beth, ill.   II. Title.
PZ7.P94965Ho   1987   [E]   86-12648
ISBN 0-688-12031-8

This is 107 Maple Street. Chrissy and Jenny live here with their mother and father, a dog named Maggie, and a fat cat named Sally.

Three hundred years ago there was no house here or even a street. There was only a forest and a bubbling spring where the animals came to drink.

One day a fierce storm roared across the forest. The sky rolled with thunder, and lightning crashed into a tree. A deer sniffed the air in alarm. Soon the woods were ablaze.

The next spring a few sturdy flowers poked through the ashes, and by the year after that the land was covered with grass. Some wildflowers grew at the edge of the stream where the deer had returned to drink.

One day the earth trembled, and a cloud of dust rose to the sky. A mighty herd of buffalo had come to eat the sweet grass and drink from the stream.

People came, following the buffalo herd. They set up their tepees near the stream, and because they liked it so much, they stayed for the whole summer.

One boy longed to be a great hunter like his father, but for now he could only pretend with his friends. In their games, one boy was chosen to be the buffalo.

His father taught the boy how to make an arrowhead and smooth it just so, the way his father had taught him. But the boy was young, and the day was hot.

He ran off to play with his friends and left the arrowhead on a rock.
When he came back later to get it, he could not find it.

The buffalo moved on, searching for new grass, and the people packed up their tepees and followed.

For a long time the land was quiet. Some rabbits made their home in the stump of a burned tree, and a fox made a den in some rocks.

One day there was a new sound. The fox looked up. A wagon train passed by, heading for California. The settlers stopped beside the stream for a night. But they dreamed of gold and places far away and were gone the next morning.

Other wagons came, following the tracks of the first. The fox family moved into the woods, but the rabbits stayed snug in their burrows until the people had gone.

Soon after, a man and a woman camped along the stream. They were heading west, but the woman would soon have a child. They looked around them and knew it was a good place to stay. The man cut down trees and made a house.

He pulled up the tree stumps left from the fire and planted his crops.
The child was a girl, and they named her Ruby and called her their
little jewel.

Ruby had a set of china dishes that she played with every day. One day when she was making a mudpie on the banks of the stream, she found an arrowhead buried deep in the ground. She put it in a cup to show her father when he came in from the fields.

Ruby's mother called her to watch the new baby. While she was gone,
a rabbit sniffed at the cup and knocked it off the rock. It fell into the tunnel
to his burrow, and the rabbit moved away to a new home under the roots
of a tree.

Ruby grew up and moved away, but her brother stayed on the farm. By now there were other people nearby, and he married a girl from another farm. They had six children, and he built a larger house so they would all fit.

Now the old wagon trail was used as a road, and the dust got into the house. When his wife complained, Ruby's brother planted a row of maple trees along the road to keep out the dust and shade the house. After the children were grown, he and his wife moved away, but one of their daughters stayed on the farm with her husband and children.

One day the children's great-aunt Ruby came for a visit. She was an old lady with snow-white hair. The children loved to hear her stories of long ago. She told them about the cup and arrowhead she had lost when she was a girl.

After she left, the children looked and looked. But they never found them, though they searched for days.

The town had grown nearly to the edge of the farm, and another man up the road filled in the stream and changed its course. For a while there was a trickle of water in the spring when the snow melted, but weeds and dirt filled in the bed, until hardly anyone remembered a stream had ever been there.

New people lived on the farm. It was the schoolteacher and his family, and they sold much of the land to others. The road was paved with bricks, so there was no longer any dust, but the maple trees remained. The branches hung down over the road, making it shady and cool. People called it Maple Street. Automobiles drove on the road, along with carts and wagons, and there were many new houses.

The house was crumbling and old, and one day some men tore it down. For a while again, the land was bare. The rabbits lived comfortably, with only an occasional owl or fox to chase them. But one day a young couple came walking along and stopped to admire the trees.

"What a wonderful place for a home," said the young woman. So they hired carpenters and masons to build a cozy house of red bricks with white trim.

The young couple lived happily in the house for several years. The young man got a job in another town, and they had to move.

The house was sold to a man and a woman who had two girls named Chrissy and Jenny and a dog named Maggie, and a fat cat named Sally.

The girls helped their father dig up a spot of ground for a garden, but it was Maggie the dog who dug up something white in the soft spring earth.
"Stop," cried Chrissy, and she picked up the tiny cup made of china. Inside was the arrowhead found and lost so long ago.

"Who lost these?" the girls wondered. Chrissy and Jenny put the cup and arrowhead on a shelf for others to see. Someday perhaps their children will play with the tiny treasures and wonder about them, too. But the cup and arrowhead will forever keep their secrets, and the children can only dream.